388,4
YEP

Yepsen, Roger

City trains:
~~~ing through
~~~ties

CITY TRAINS

Moving through America's Cities by Rail

CITY TRAINS

Moving through America's Cities by Rail

Roger Yepsen

Macmillan Publishing Company   New York

Maxwell Macmillan Canada   Toronto

Maxwell Macmillan International
New York   Oxford   Singapore   Sydney

In memory of Bill Burdell,
who took me on my first city trains
under New York
and out into the New Jersey countryside

—R.Y.

*Title page photo: In busy cities, trains are forced to burrow under the
ground and to travel above it. This train rolls on elevated tracks in Boston.*

Macmillan Publishing Company is part of the Maxwell Communication Group of Companies.
Macmillan Publishing Company, 866 Third Avenue, New York, NY 10022
Maxwell Macmillan Canada, Inc., 1200 Eglinton Avenue East, Suite 200
Don Mills, Ontario M3C 3N1 First edition
Printed in the United States of America

10 9 8 7 6 5 4 3 2 1

The text of this book is set in 13 point ITC Garamond Light.
Book design by Constance Ftera

Library of Congress Cataloging-in-Publication Data
Yepsen, Roger B.
City trains : moving through America's cities by rail /
Roger Yepsen. — 1st ed.
p.   cm.
Includes bibliographical references and index.
Summary: An illustrated history of the various types of public transportation used in cities
including horsecars, streetcars, trolleys, interurbans, cable cars, subways, light rails, and monorails.
ISBN 0-02-793675-9
1. Street-railroads—United States—Juvenile literature.
2. Subways—United States—Juvenile literature.
[1. Street-railroads. 2. Subways. 3. Transportation. 4. City and town life.] I. Title.
HE4451.Y46 1993   388.4'2'0973—dc20   92-2395

CONTENTS

CHAPTER 1

A Good Way to Move People

How far from home will you walk today? To school, perhaps. Or maybe to a store or a friend's.

Chances are, it will be a short distance. And for most of human history, that's how small a person's world tended to be. Walking was the only ride. Towns didn't grow much broader than a person could walk. Shops and industries and schools stayed small, too, because each could be reached by only a limited number of people on foot.

Above: Early city trains had no sides—a pleasant feature when riding through parkland like this.

The world stayed a cozy place until the early 1800s. That's when a simple invention—metal wheels rolling on metal rails—changed the way people spread across this planet.

It was as if the human race had grown wings. Instead of walking at three miles per hour, we could roll at sixty. Carts and coaches already had been hooked up to horses, of course. But these vehicles rarely traveled much faster than a walk. The streets wouldn't allow it. Rain turned dirt streets into pudding. And paved streets, with their cobblestones shaped like loaves of bread, were too bouncy.

Rails made the difference. They were so smooth and level that people could move much faster and farther. Towns blossomed into big cities. (Another couple of inventions helped cities to grow, too: Iron skeletons allowed buildings to rise into the sky, and elevators, like small up-and-down trains, made these tall buildings practical.)

The new cities were great not only in size, but in what they could do. They became home to great artists and great art museums, great sports teams, great publishers, great colleges, and great corporations, all depending on many people living and working in a concentrated area.

The first trains weren't all that speedy. But to a person who had never gone much faster than a walk, they must have been as exciting as space exploration is to us. There was a popular theory that if you traveled much faster than a horse's gallop, you might explode!

But before long, city people were riding trains *in* the streets, in tunnels *below* the streets, and on platforms arching high *over* the streets. If you walked a couple of blocks in any direction, there would be a train to take you downtown or out into the countryside or clear across the continent.

Streetcars, subways, cable cars, inclined-plane railroads, elevated railroads, interurban railroads—never in history had there been such convenient and affordable ways to travel. And that's not all. When you look closely at old, browning photographs of these city trains, you get the impression that the passengers were having fun.

It's early morning in Lancaster, Pennsylvania, and a group of factory workers and their families are ready to roll out of town for a picnic in the countryside.

CHAPTER 2

Horsecars

It has always been easier to travel *between* cities than *inside* them. By the mid-1800s, steam railroads were whisking people across the countryside at a mile a minute. And yet in town, traffic crawled no faster than centuries before. The rich could flag down a horse-drawn cab, or ride in their own elegant carriages. But for everyone else, the choices were simple: Either climb aboard a plodding horse-drawn coach, called an omnibus, or walk.

Above: Mules on the Ontario, California, street railway were given a free ride downhill to save their strength for the next climb.

Then came the horse-drawn railroad car, known as a horsecar—"the greatest achievement of man," boasted the mayor of New York at the opening of his city's first line. This achievement was pretty, as inventions go. The cars were hand-made of wood, and decorated with the care you might take with an Easter egg. Unlike today's railroad equipment, almost any bright color was considered appropriate, and decorations included paintings of famous people and historical scenes. Cars were even given names, as has always been traditional for ships. Horsecar companies took pride in their horses, too. One company distinguished itself from the rest by using only gray steeds—hundreds of them. It sent agents out into the countryside to buy powerful gray horses wherever they could be found.

Not everyone loved the new horsecars. Drivers of old-fashioned omnibuses didn't appreciate the competition. They threw stones at horsecars and tried to block their tracks. Wagon drivers complained, too. They were afraid that horsecars would begin carrying freight as well as people. To reassure them, some city governments ruled that the new rails must be spaced exactly 5 feet, 2¼ inches apart—most horse-drawn wagons had wheels that far apart, so they also could benefit from the smoother ride.

Horsecar railways earned other enemies when they brushed snow from their tracks in winter. That made the streets rough traveling for horse-drawn sleighs. Some cities prohibited the railways from clearing the tracks when the sleighing was good. Still other people claimed the new cars were too dangerous. A New York newspaper reported that the horsecar lines of the city were killing an average of one person a week.

But the horsecars continued to roll. They became the most important type of transportation in North America's cities, with hundreds of companies running 18,000 cars over several thousand miles of track.

Not everyone was free to climb aboard and have a seat. In many cities, African Americans had to stand out on the front platform, exposed to rain, snow, and cold.

A horsecar rounds a sharp corner in New York. In the mid-nineteenth century, muscle power was just about the only way around the huge city—either a horse's, or your own.

The Trouble with Horses

Horsecars were too big a success for their own good. So many were put on the tracks that they jammed the streets, losing their great advantage—speed. New York's horsecars were taking well over an hour to roll just five miles. An energetic person on the sidewalk could *walk* nearly that fast. Sharp minds began thinking of other locations for the rails.

City trains could be run below the streets, although tunneling was a new and dangerous science. Trains could also be run in the air, on land bridges. But a more immediate answer to traffic jams was to find a replacement for the horse.

The street railways of North America were pulled by 100,000 animals. Horses were friendly and familiar. But they had their problems. Horses were slow. It took a couple of them to pull most cars, or a team of four if the line was very hilly. And their workday was only half as long as that of the human driver. Nevertheless, they worked up quite an appetite and ate thirty pounds of hay and grain every day.

Cities had to put up with mountains of manure (more than ten pounds a day per animal) and lakes of urine (the streets couldn't be paved with blacktop because horse urine destroyed it). The horses themselves weren't cheap. A good one cost between 125 and 250 dollars—the equivalent of what a new car might cost today! And yet most horses were retired after just three to five years of work. (There were exceptions, though. Old Crooked Tail, a horse that began pulling cars of the Chicago City Railway at the ripe old age of five, worked every day for another twenty-one years. All together, Old Crooked Tail's trips roughly equaled the distance from the earth to the moon.)

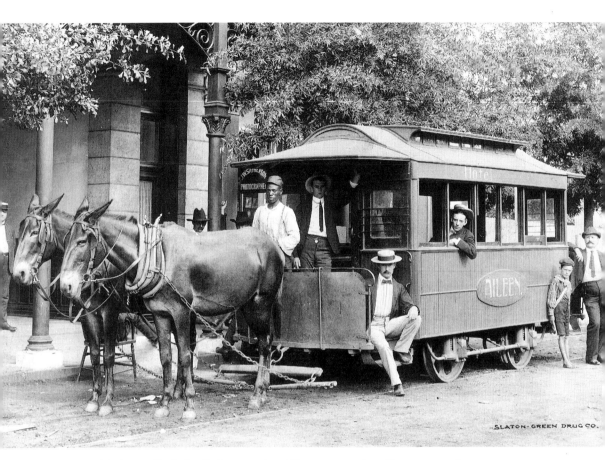

Mules pulled the little wooden Aileen *over the dirt streets of Washington, Georgia. When this photo was taken, in 1908, horsecars were just a memory in all but a few cities.*

Finally, horses could get very sick. In 1872, an epidemic killed or disabled 18,000 horses in New York alone. There had to be a better way to move people.

A number of cities tried sticking tiny steam engines in the cars. But these cars were hot, clumsy, smoky, and frightening to horses sharing the street. They were called dummies; the name sounds like an insult, but in fact it came about because

14

they were disguised as regular cars to try to avoid scaring horses. The dummies puffed about the streets for a few years before being cut up for scrap.

Horses weren't the best way to pull city trains. Neither was steam. The most suitable form of power was one that could be drawn into the railway along spidery strands of metal—electricity.

This horseless horsecar was pulled down the streets of Baltimore by the electric dummy engine (an advance over earlier steam dummies) on the left.

CHAPTER 3

Cable Railroads

Inventors worked hard to find a replacement for the most troublesome part of the horsecar, the horse. An electric motor seemed to be the best answer. It was quiet and didn't belch smoke—good manners a coal-burning steam engine didn't happen to have.

But for much of the 1800s, electricity was looked upon as a slightly tamer form of lightning. Could it be safely sent out to operate cars around town? Few cities even had electric streetlights.

Above: The world's first cable cars climbed Clay Street hill in San Francisco.

While inventors figured out how to get power to city trains, another idea came along: Use a steam engine, but stick it in a building and use it to pull cars on a long cable. In that way, the noise and smoke could be kept off the streets.

These cable cars were a lot like that indoor vehicle, the elevator. In fact, the first successful cable railroad was dreamed up by a man who happened to manufacture wire for elevators.

A Violent Inspiration

The man's name was Andrew Hallidie, and his idea was inspired by a terrible horsecar accident. He watched as a team of four horses struggled to pull its car up a steep, slippery San Francisco hill. One of the horses tripped, and the car began sliding backward. In desperation, the driver spun the brake wheel. But a part snapped. The car continued sliding, out of control now and dragging the horses behind it. When the car finally came to a halt, the animals were so badly injured that they had to be killed.

It occurred to Hallidie that if a cable was trusted to lift elevators, it could haul cars safely up the city's steepest streets. After testing his idea, he opened the first San Francisco cable-car line in 1873.

If you've ever watched clothes travel back and forth along a clothesline on pulleys, you understand how a cable car works. Instead of shirts and pants, wooden streetcars were attached to the line. The line itself was a loop of wire cable, up to several thousand feet long, that traveled in a slot in the street. The cable was pulled by a coal-burning steam engine in a powerhouse at one end of the tracks. The engine turned a huge spool that continually reeled in one strand of cable while letting out the other strand.

Cable cars weren't large, but they needed two-person crews. The "gripman" was kept busy working a lever that grabbed or let go of the constantly moving cable under the street. He also controlled the brakes, stepped on a pedal to drop sand on slippery rails for better braking, and rang the warning bell at every corner. The conductor collected tickets or money and notified the gripman to start or stop by ringing a special bell. (More than once, an impatient passenger rang this bell when the conductor stepped into a shop for a quick errand, fooling the gripman and forcing the conductor to chase after his moving car.)

Cable cars caught on with riders because they were two to three times faster than horsecars. They went still faster if the gripman dared to "skin the cable," letting go of the cable to plummet downhill. Passengers also had a thrilling ride when a car got snared in the cable and couldn't be stopped. The car raced along, frantically ringing its bell as a warning. One by one, the cable cars ahead were forced to join the high-speed parade in order to avoid being smashed from behind. Eventually, someone would call the powerhouse to shut down the line.

Adventuresome children took advantage of the constantly moving cable. They tied a rope to a wagon and dangled the other end in the cable slot until it was snared. Then they jumped aboard for a free and *dangerous* ride—there was no way to stop. If police spotted them, the kids cut the rope, grabbed the wagon, and ran away.

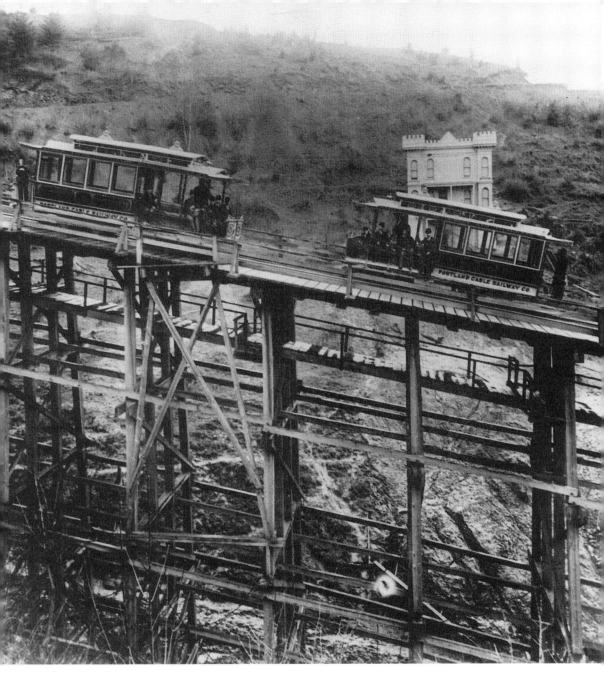

Cable car passengers must have held their breath on this line serving Portland, Oregon: It was the second steepest ever built in the United States.

A car climbs San Francisco's Hyde Street hill. This is the sort of slope that inspired Andrew Hallidie to design his cable car system.

The Cable Car Goes Downhill

Americans tend to become bored with yesterday's marvels. By 1900, one newspaper was already comparing the cable car with the dinosaur, suggesting that the railways would soon be extinct. In fact, within six years, all but thirty miles of cable lines were abandoned. The companies had trouble making money. Each car needed a two-person crew. And the long metal cables, being far heavier than the cars themselves, put a tremendous drain on the powerhouse motors. Another type of city train, the electric streetcar, was cheaper to run.

The companies that lasted the longest happened to serve cities with big hills—Tacoma and Seattle, in Washington State, and San Francisco, which continues to operate just four miles of its lines. San Francisco's cable cars are probably the most famous city trains in the world. But they are more of a museum exhibit than a true part of the city's transportation system. Still, the cable cars have become a symbol of San Francisco, and tourists love to ride them.

Inclined-Plane Railroads

The steepest tracks of all are those of the inclined-plane railroads. They operate like cable cars, but travel up difficult

The cars of Pittsburgh's Duquesne Incline were originally built as horsecars back in 1873. They are thought to be the oldest transit vehicles in regular use anywhere in the world.

hills that no other vehicles could manage. Most railways climb hills gradually, by turning this way and that on a long and winding track. An inclined-plane railway goes straight up. The route is shorter, but so steep that a self-powered car would have great trouble either starting up or slowing down.

An incline typically has two tracks and runs two cars at a time—one up, the other down. Both cars are connected to a drum in the powerhouse at the top of the line. The weight of the downward car makes it relatively easy for an electric motor in the powerhouse to lift the upward car. More than thirty inclines were once used in the United States and Canada.

Pittsburgh, nestled in a mountainous landscape, had more incline railways than any other city. Huge industries lined river valleys in the heart of town, and employees needed a way to reach their jobs from homes in the hills high above. The city continues to make good use of two lines.

One of them is the Duquesne Inclined Plane Company. It operated for ninety years before having to be shut down because of worn parts. The Boy Scouts were among the local groups that helped raise money to get the line moving again. The little cars still have their cherry paneling and bird's-eye maple trim. They look like museum pieces, and yet manage to carry half a million riders a year. The railroad has to pay roughly a dime of accident insurance for every rider, even though there isn't a safer transportation system in North America—no one has died or been seriously injured on it since 1873.

Not far from Pittsburgh, an inclined railway serves Johnstown, Pennsylvania. Its cars are huge. Back in the 1890s, they carried wagons and horses as well as people. From the 1930s

Johnstown's inclined railway carries automobiles as well as passengers. The lone person on this car seems to want to avoid the dizzying view.

through the 1950s, they carried city buses. Today, automobiles are the biggest load. The Johnstown line is said to be the steepest ever built, and the city is proud of its railway. The track is outlined at night with white lights; the bulbs are changed to red and green at Christmas, and orange at Halloween.

CHAPTER 4

Streetcars

The horse was finally knocked off the streets of America by a metal can filled with magnets and wire—the electric motor. It was quiet and powerful. It was small enough to tuck under the floor of a railcar. And it didn't make a mess in the road.

Inventors had been playing around with electric motors for decades. Vermont blacksmith Thomas Davenport built the first successful American electric train back in 1835. But it was a toy, too small to haul people.

Half a century of tinkering went by until an inventor, Frank

Above: Steam railroads lost many passengers to trolleys, and often refused to let trolley companies cross their tracks. This Massachusetts trolley solved the problem by leaping right over the railroad in its way.

25

Sprague, turned the electric motor into something more than a fascinating gimmick. Sprague designed an electric streetcar line for Richmond, Virginia, and the quiet cars caught the attention of cities across the continent. Within just three years, two hundred streetcar systems were built either by Sprague or to his plans.

Streetcars were faster than horsecars. And they harnessed the mysterious force that caused the sky to thunder. Still, it's hard for us to look back and understand the excitement that surrounded these little trains. They seemed *poky*, not speedy. That's because they looked like old-fashioned coaches without the horses.

The cars were put together by hand from wood, just as horse-drawn vehicles always had been. They borrowed the curved sides and arch-topped windows of stage coaches. The motorman stood on an open platform through all four seasons. In rain, he would wear a fisherman's oilskin suit and high rubber boots, as if he were on the deck of a ship at sea.

Perhaps because they were faster than they looked, streetcars tended to sneak up on people. President Theodore Roosevelt was injured when a car of a Massachusetts line hit his carriage and threw him to the ground. Pedestrians darted in front of cars, underestimating their speed. Or they made the mistake of standing between pairs of tracks, in what was called the devil's strip, as cars passed on either side. To catch potential

The first streetcars were a popular hit in cities across the country.
A Philadelphia newspaper printed this build-it-yourself cardboard trolley,
complete with motorman and conductor. (To construct your own
model, make a larger copy of this page, glue it to poster board, then
just follow the instructions.)

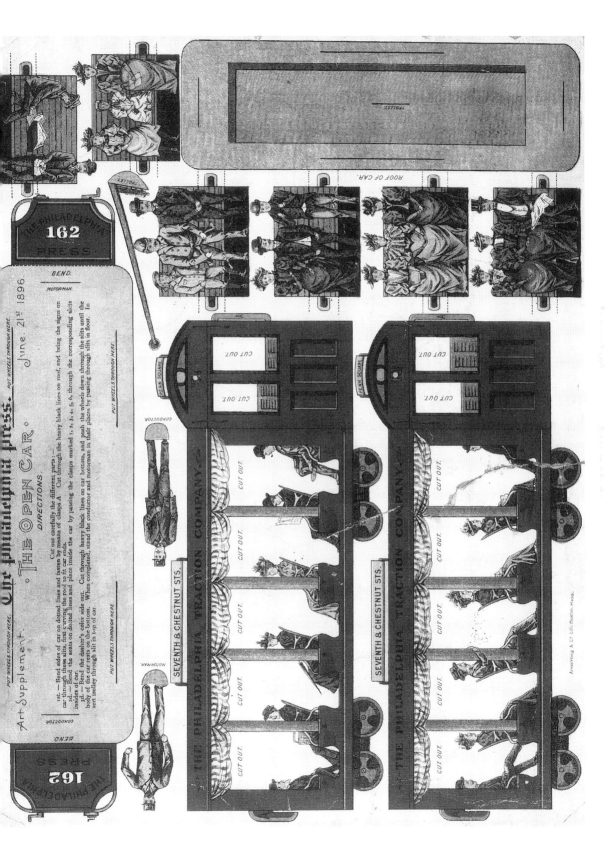

The Philadelphia Press

162

THE PHILADELPHIA PRESS

PUT WHEELS THROUGH HERE.

Art Supplement.

·THE OPEN CAR·

June 21st 1896.

DIRECTIONS

Cut out carefully the different parts:—

1st.— Bend sides of car on dotted lines and fasten by means of clasps A   Cut through the heavy black lines on roof, and bring the signs on car through these slits, first curving the rod to fit car ends.   Cut through the heavy black lines on roof, and bring the signs on inside of car.   and place the seats on dotted lines and place inside the car by passing the clasps A by passing the clasps marked 1, 2, 3, 4, 5, 6, through the corresponding slits

2d.— Bend the dasher's color side out.   Cut through heavy black lines on car bottom, and push the wheels down through the slits until the body of the car rests on the bottom.   When completed, stand the conductor and motorman in their places by passing through slits in door.   In sert trolley through slit in top of car.

PUT WHEELS THROUGH HERE.

PUT WHEELS THROUGH HERE.

PUT WHEELS THROUGH HERE.

BEND.

MOTORMAN.

CONDUCTOR.

BEND.

THE PHILADELPHIA TRACTION COMPANY.

SEVENTH & CHESTNUT STS.

THE PHILADELPHIA TRACTION COMPANY.

SEVENTH & CHESTNUT STS.

CONDUCTOR.

MOTORMAN.

CUT OUT.   CUT OUT.   CUT OUT.   CUT OUT.   CUT OUT.

CUT OUT.   CUT OUT.   CUT OUT.   CUT OUT.   CUT OUT.

PENN SQUARE.

PENN SQUARE.

CUT OUT.

CUT OUT.

CUT OUT.

CUT OUT.

ROOF OF CAR.

TROLLEY.

TROLLEY.

Armstrong & Co. Lith. Boston, Mass.

victims just before they slipped under the wheels, many trolleys had little trampolines, called safety fenders, mounted on their front ends.

The citizens of Brooklyn, New York, were known as trolley dodgers because streetcars filled their streets. The local baseball team picked up the nickname, eventually dropping *trolley*. Years later, as you may know, the Dodgers moved to Los Angeles.

The insides of the first streetcars were old-fashioned, too.

Steam locomotives had cowcatchers on the front end, and streetcars had people catchers. This car was a post office, in which clerks sorted mail as they rolled through town.
(New York Transit Archives, Brooklyn, N.Y.)

Some young people were tempted to hitch free rides on streetcars.
It was a dangerous practice, and one railway staged this photograph
to help discourage hitching.

They seemed as cozy as the rooms of a house, with varnished wooden walls and paintings of landscapes and flowers. Colored-glass windows just below the roof, called clerestories, helped to ventilate the cars. The color of the glass was a clue to which line the car traveled—a big help to passengers who could not read destination signs.

Streetcars in Summer and Winter

In summer, open-sided cars made use of the free breeze. One streetcar company installed fans for the comfort of summertime passengers—but only to make them *imagine* they were cooler, since the fans had no motors and could only whirl in the wind like pinwheels!

Streetcars were not so pleasant in winter. A single coal stove made passengers feel either frozen or cooked, depending on where they sat—that is, if the cars were heated at all. Many streetcar lines simply scattered hay on the floor to help insulate passengers' feet. Gradually, cars were equipped with electric heaters, but the heat often was switched off to spare enough power to run extra cars during rush hours. The heaters weren't a match for northern winters. When reporters of a Philadelphia newspaper climbed aboard the city's trolleys with thermometers, they found temperatures ranging from thirty-four to forty-one degrees Fahrenheit in cars *with* electric heat, and below freezing in those without.

Because streetcars were among the first popular inventions to run on electricity, many lines had to make their own. They burned coal to produce steam, and the steam spun generators that sent electricity to the cars. In most cities, trolleys drew their electricity from overhead wires that were draped over the street like telephone lines. But when streetcars came to Washington, D.C., overhead lines weren't allowed to clutter the streets of the nation's capital. So as each trolley from outside of town reached the city limits, the pole that picked up the current was taken down, and the car was hooked up to a plow that took its electricity from a trough under the street.

The plow sounds like a good idea. But it was troublesome. In one of the worst imaginable jobs, a man was stationed in a pit under the streets to remove and install plows as cars passed the city border. Summer temperatures could make the trough expand, pinch the plow, and stop the car. And passengers were often stranded at the scene of a fire because the cars couldn't travel past the fire hoses. In other cities, long portable bridges known as jumpers were laid down to allow streetcars to travel up and over these obstructions. But there was no way for a Washington car to get its plow over the hoses.

The Streetcar Craze

Streetcars changed the way Americans traveled. By 1902, there were 22,000 miles of track in the streets of the United States. The little cars carried five billion passengers a year— more than seven times the tickets sold by all of the nation's steam railroads.

Streetcars also changed the way America looked. They al-

This streetcar is rolling over a pair of portable hump-backed rails called "jumpers," to avoid chopping the firemen's hoses like strands of spaghetti. (Photo from *Rails in Richmond*, by Carlton N. McKenney.)

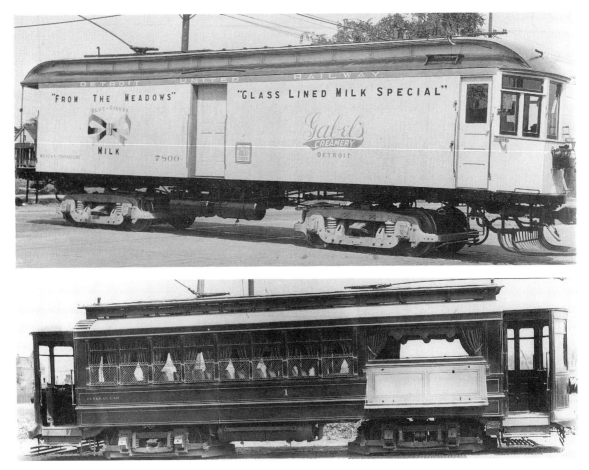

Top: Streetcars helped bring milk from the farm to the city.

Middle: This funeral car took both casket and mourners to cemetaries along the streetcar lines of Chicago.

Left: This streetcar snowplow sat out the summer, waiting for winter's storms.

lowed people to move quickly and easily, so cities were able to expand as never before. In 1880, before the trolley came along, a city typically would grow as wide as its horsecars traveled—just four miles or so. Only twenty U.S. cities had more than 100,000 people. But the electric streetcar traveled farther and faster. By 1910, another thirty cities had topped 100,000. And that wasn't counting the thousands of people who spilled over the city borders into the brand-new communities known as suburbs.

Streetcar lines did more than carry people. In many cities, they also acted as rolling mailboxes. Anyone could drop a letter into a box attached to a passing streetcar, and the mail would be delivered when the car happened by the post office. Some cars were rolling post offices themselves. These trolleys, usually painted an eye-catching white and gold, roved around the city picking up mail. Clerks were on board to sort the mail the instant it was picked up. That reduced the time it took a letter to get to its destination.

Other cars carried packages, milk, and heavier items, acting like tiny freight trains. In fact, trolley operators found they often could make more money hauling *things* than people, and they took over much freight business that had continued to be handled by horse-drawn stagecoaches and wagons. Streetcar companies hauled coffins, too. Handsome black funeral cars had upholstered benches on which the mourners sat in comfort, and shades could be pulled down for privacy. The coffin traveled in its own section of the car.

Canada had its share of unusual trolleys. Montreal used steel-plated streetcars to carry prisoners to the city's courthouse. In Edmonton, Alberta, a streetcar library visited the

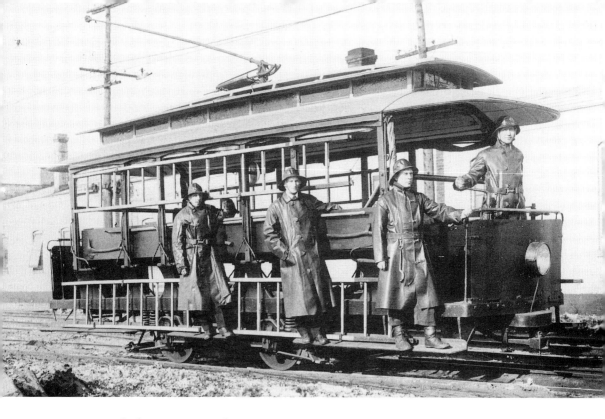

Duluth, Minnesota, firemen pose proudly on their streetcar. It was used to fight fires on a point of land that had tracks but no road.

town's neighborhoods. And in Toronto each summer, "bathing cars" took kids to the shore of Lake Ontario—no tickets needed.

Streetcar companies discovered a great way to sell more tickets—build an amusement park way out in the countryside so that nearly everyone would have to ride a trolley to get there.

These parks were the Disney Worlds of their day. In Chicago, streetcars took thrill seekers to Ferris Wheel Park, named for its famous ride—the biggest Ferris wheel in the world. Its gondolas reached 250 feet above the ground, and riders enjoyed (or were terrified by) the fifty-mile view. Another attraction, the world's largest artificially frozen skating pond, drew trolley riders to a park along the Pittsburgh Railway.

Trolleys in Trouble

Streetcars were the perfect form of transportation, it seemed. The quick little trolleys would clang through the streets forever.

But nothing is forever when it comes to transportation. There is always a new and improved vehicle ready to appear around the corner. And so it was that streetcars found themselves sitting like turtles in an impatient tide of automobiles and buses. The squat, unsteerable vehicles had become the slowpokes of the streets. Cleveland's handsome green-and-gray streetcars had to be painted bright colors so that speedy automobiles wouldn't keep running into them. The streetcar had become old-fashioned.

By the 1920s, streetcar companies began to rip up track. Once-proud trolleys looked like shacks on wheels. And trolley amusement parks were having trouble amusing crowds year after year. As families bought cars, they discovered other places to spend their free time and money. The parks closed by the hundreds, to be replaced by housing developments or weeds.

The streetcar companies themselves had helped chase away passengers. That's because trolleys allowed people to settle out in the countryside in new suburban communities. And for all of their strengths, trains aren't very good at serving people who are scattered over the landscape. That job is better suited to cars and buses. They can go anyplace, not just where the tracks lead.

A Better Streetcar

The streetcar was an endangered vehicle. In 1929, trolley companies and manufacturers got together to dream up a better streetcar, one that could draw passengers back to city rails. After five years of work, this Presidents' Conference Committee came up with a lightweight, all-steel trolley with a streamlined appearance. Inside, there were cushioned seats and improved heating. The ride was quieter and smoother, as people had come to expect from rubber-tired cars and buses.

Thousands of these cars—called PCCs, after the name of the committee—were built between 1934 and 1952. They were so attractive and dependable that a surprising number are still in daily use today. Because of the careful planning that went into them, they don't run or look like near antiques.

The world's longest streetcar line—thirteen miles—is still running in Philadelphia. The PCC car shown here had a streamlined nose, more to make it look *faster than to help it actually* move *faster.*

On the busier lines, the new streetcars held their own. They could carry more passengers per hour than a string of smoky buses. And as World War II began, there were lots of passengers to be carried. Gasoline sales had been limited to conserve energy for the war effort, and few new automobiles were built. That meant millions more travelers for the trolleys.

But when the war was over, these riders went back to their cars. The streetcars again found themselves caught in the traffic, and cities continued to rip out their streetcar tracks. The competition from buses and cars was just too stiff, people said. But there have been rumors of other reasons. Of murder.

Some transportation experts believe there was a plot to do away with the streetcar. A company named National City Lines had been buying streetcar systems around the United States. But it wasn't interested in running trolleys, according to this theory. Its goal was to destroy them. In city after city, the company would replace the street railways with buses. In Philadelphia alone, more than thirty lines were ripped up forever, and buses appeared where the trolleys had been.

What did the company have against streetcars? It happened to be run by General Motors, the biggest automobile and bus manufacturer in the world; by huge oil companies; and by the Firestone tire company. The faster the streetcar was banished from the cities, the more products these firms could expect to sell.

The Federal Bureau of Investigation looked into National City Lines, and the company was taken to court by the federal government. After trials dragged on for eight years, the companies were declared guilty. But they were fined just one thousand dollars each. That was a slap on the wrist, you could say,

In cities across North America, thousands of old streetcars were burned like fallen leaves. A few were saved, for use as diners or cottages.

for an illegal plan that probably had earned them tens of millions. The officers of the companies were fined, too—a dollar apiece.

Of the hundreds of North American cities that once ran streetcars, just nine held on through the 1960s, and they continue to use them today. They are Boston, Cleveland, Mexico City, Newark, New Orleans, Philadelphia, Pittsburgh, San Francisco, and Toronto. Why did these few lines survive? Most were lucky to travel tracks that were at least partly off the road; because these trolleys didn't have to tangle with cars, they could travel faster. In some cities, the trolley has been given a new name—light-rail vehicle, or LRV—to suggest that it still can be a practical way to travel (see page 58).

New Old Trolleys

Streetcars are cute, quiet, and fun to ride. Many cities have rediscovered them as a way to entice shoppers away from the suburban malls and back into town.

Sometimes old trolleys are brought back to life. But these ancient cars are hard to find. American cities have been shopping for them as far away as Australia. Now, a company in Iowa has begun reproducing trolleys, just as they were made a hundred years ago.

Unlike a bus, an open streetcar seems to invite people to climb aboard. Realizing that, cities are ordering brand new streetcars like this one to serve their downtown shopping districts.

CHAPTER 5

Did you ever travel 80 miles an hour? On your next trip to Milwaukee use CHICAGO NORTH SHORE & MILWAUKEE R.R. Trains every hour on the hour

Interurbans

There may never have been a more pleasant way to travel than in an interurban car. There may never be again.

These little trains were so nice to ride that many tickets were bought by passengers who had no particular place to go. Teenagers dated on them, out of sight of parents. Others rode on doctor's orders, to relax in order to sleep better at night. In summer, when the interurbans ran open-sided cars, people took a spin just to cool off.

On weekends, entire families piled on and went out into the country. Trolley companies published booklets of places to

Above: Thanks to awful highways, interurbans could travel much faster than early automobiles—a point that the North Shore interurban rubbed in with this highway billboard.

visit along the tracks. And the open cars were excellent for sightseeing—a lot like going on a hayride through forests and fields. Although open cars didn't travel very fast, even twenty miles per hour seemed like an adventure in a car without sides.

Riding an Interurban

Each new breath of wind carried a different scent—of new-mown hay, honeysuckle, freshly turned earth. From the perfume of spring flowers until the open cars were put away in leaf-burning season, the smells changed with the changing landscape.

It was a countryside free of billboards and gas stations and shopping centers. These additions to our world came later, when the automobile won the hearts of the interurban's passengers.

But interurban railroads weren't just for fun. They really did go to important places. In fact, their destination was in the name. *Interurban* was a new word pieced together from an old language, Latin, meaning that the trains traveled between cities.

An interurban train led two lives. One was as a city citizen, slowly tracing through the streets like a streetcar. But at the edge of town, these electric cars became athletes, leaving the road and breaking into a sprint through the countryside. A few could approach a hundred miles per hour.

For pocket change, an interurban car would stop outside your home and take you to your destination. (Or *almost* take you there—a vehicle on rails can never be as flexible as one that's able to turn right up your driveway.) Most lines didn't go farther than fifty miles, but it was possible to string together long trips along the rails of several companies. The longest trip ever charted went from Elkhart Lake, Wisconsin, all the way to Oneonta, New York—although there is no practical reason anyone would want to have endured this 1,087-mile trip on cars that didn't serve food or have bathrooms!

In New England, $2.40 in nickels would take you on a ride along a dozen interurbans from Boston to New York City. Again, this twenty-hour ride over the lines of a dozen railroads seems more of a marathon run than a pleasant thing to do. Steam railroads zipped between the two cities in a quarter of the time. And yet, people were fascinated by how far they could go with a few coins. A 1917 traveler's guide told "Mr. and Mrs. Trolleyist" how to make the trip. The booklet suggested where to stop for "sodas and ice cream to cool the parched throat of the summer trolleyer," and described such trackside wonders as the biggest boulder in the world (ten thousand tons) and the lake with the longest name (Chargoggagogmanchoggagogg).

A Bigger, Faster Streetcar

Were interurban trolleys any different from the streetcars that hung around town? Yes, although a quick glance at the photographs on these pages might not suggest why.

Interurban cars were heavier, for better handling and greater safety at high speed. With two to five times as much

A map from the 1917 edition of Trolley Trips through New England *showed the many routes a person could wander aboard interurban cars. Within just twenty years, all but a few scraps of this track had vanished.*

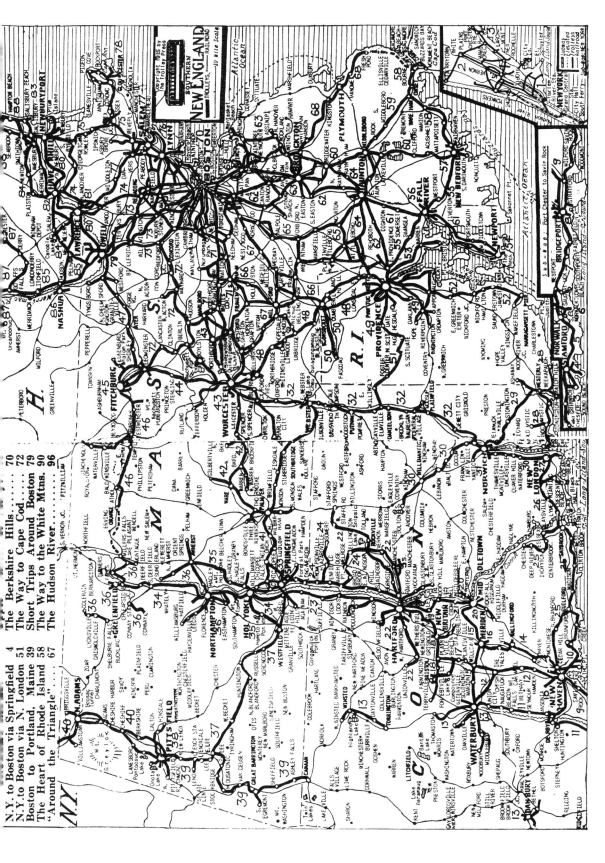

power, they could travel much faster than streetcars. Interurban seats were often upholstered for comfort, like those on long-distance steam trains. In fact, some interurbans were just like the short-distance trains of steam railroads, except that they used electricity, entered town in the streets, and typically ran few if any freight trains on their tracks.

In the city, an interurban cautiously rang its bell just like a streetcar. But as the clutter of the city was left behind, the motorman switched on a more powerful headlight and used a loud railroad air whistle to chase people and animals from the tracks. The interurban didn't stop for traffic at country roads—it barreled right through.

Interurbans could be found in most states, but they were plentiful only in the Northeast and Midwest and along the Pacific Coast. Ohio and Indiana had the most. The interurban was especially appreciated by isolated farm families, and in these two states, few towns of more than five thousand people were without intercity trolleys.

The Steam Railroads Get Nervous

An interurban car didn't come complete with passengers—many of the people in the seats were taken from another form of transportation. The losers were the stagecoach and short-distance trains of the steam railroads.

Stage companies couldn't hope to compete with the interurban—the horse, having been driven from the cities by streetcars, now lost its last transportation job to the interurban trolley.

But the steam railroads put up a fight. There had been bad

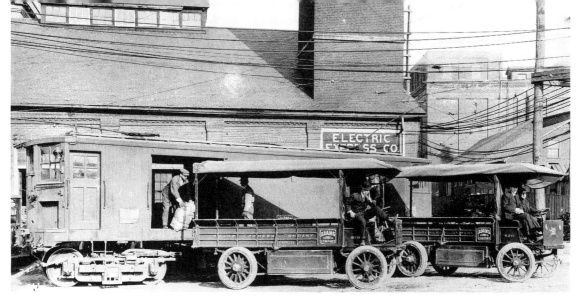

Interurban lines were built to carry people, but they also carried freight to and from businesses along the routes.

feelings between steam and electric lines from the very first days of railroading in the 1830s. When an electric locomotive was built as an experiment in Scotland, crews from nearby steam locomotives promptly tore it apart.

The interurbans were greeted in much the same way. If they tried to cross the tracks of steam railroads, these larger, older companies often went to court to stop construction. Or, steam railroad crews would simply rip up the interurban's new track—and swing their fists, if necessary. The construction gang of the new Ohio Central interurban was attacked by men from the two largest steam railroads in the United States, the New York Central and the Pennsylvania. In California, a railroad crew sprayed interurban tracklayers with a locomotive's live steam to stop their work.

But the interurbans couldn't be stopped. If they weren't able to get permission to cross a railroad's tracks, they could toss up a bridge and make the crossing in midair.

The Dream Interurban

Every town wanted its interurban line, and far too much track was laid. For example, even though six steam railroads already linked Kansas City and Saint Joseph, Missouri, an optimistic interurban company went ahead and laid its own tracks between the cities. A few interurbans lasted just a year before going out of business.

The most optimistic interurban of all declared it would build a 75-mile-per-hour line from Chicago to New York. A number of steam railroads already offered dozens of daily trains between the two cities. But that didn't discourage the Chicago–New York Electric Air Line Railroad. The company said it would beat the competition by traveling straight as an arrow, without curves or hills to slow its trolleys.

There were a few obvious problems with this plan. One of them was the Appalachian Mountains. They happened to lie squarely in the way. The Air Line's planners explained they would tunnel right through. And what about the danger of running 75-mile-per-hour trains over crossings with public roads and other railroads? The Air Line, true to its name, planned to build bridges over them all.

The greatest interurban of them all began laying its cross-country track in a little town called South La Porte, Indiana. After spending four years and all of its money, the company had managed to go just fifteen miles. Its dizzy idealism was to blame. True to the promise to avoid hills, the tracks eased up a mile-long ramp of earth simply to cross another railroad. And then the line reached Coffey Creek, the little stream that broke the company's back. To keep from dipping the track into the creek's valley, a mountain of dirt—180 feet wide at the base and two miles long—was built to support the rails.

The Air Line ran for a few more years over its scrap of track, then went out of business. You still can see the huge fills today, rising above the flat Indiana landscape. They serve as monuments to how humans can be carried away with technology.

Trolley Parks

Interurban cars were busiest at weekday rush hours, and traffic was apt to be light the rest of the time. To lure more people to ride when the cars were emptiest—evenings and weekends—many interurbans followed the example of the streetcar companies and built picnic grounds and amusement parks along the tracks. People bought tickets not only for roller

Many interurban companies built amusement parks out in the country to attract passengers. This line ran to Glen Rock Park, just outside Wilkes-Barre, Pennsylvania. The cars only look as though they're about to travel right up the roller coaster.

coasters and Ferris wheels, but for the trolleys themselves, in order to reach the park.

One of the finest interurban spots was the Chicago and North Shore Railroad's Ravinia Park, north of Evanston, Illinois. The North Shore was often called the finest interurban of them all, and its park was no mere playground with penny rides and booths offering teddy bear prizes. Its landscaped grounds included the outdoor theater that became the summer home of the Chicago Symphony Orchestra. People would take specially scheduled cars out to the park, listen to the performance, and have a light supper as they rolled home.

The big attraction at Castle Rock Park, an hour's ride west of Philadelphia, was the rocks. Children climbed over them, playing hide-and-seek. Adults were interested in the rocks, too, but for another reason. It was said that a modern-day Robin Hood named Sandy Flash had hidden a treasure among the rocks. Just where, no one knew, because Flash had been hanged for his thievery. The money never turned up. When people lost interest in the park and its hidden treasure, the practical-minded trolley company crushed the attraction into gravel for the track beds!

Eating and Sleeping on a Trolley

Interurban companies weren't large, but they did their best to run cars that were just as handsome and comfortable as the famous first-class "limiteds" of the steam railroads.

A limited train usually limits two things. It makes only a few stops, to permit traveling at a faster average speed. And certain cars are limited to those who are willing to pay an extra

48

Above: For passengers who enjoyed the view from a porch, the Jamestown, Westfield and Northwestern ran trolleys with observation platforms. Though only a few miles long, this interurban line proudly proclaimed itself "America's Scenic Route."

Below: Interurbans did whatever they could to make passengers comfortable. This sleeping car offered beds to overnight travelers on Indiana's Interstate lines.

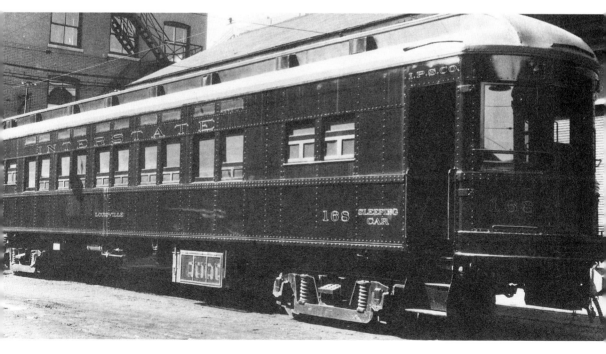

charge for the privilege of riding the train. On an interurban, what did passengers get for the additional five to twenty-five cents? The limiteds of the North Shore offered lounge cars with armchairs and a radio, and parlor-buffet cars staffed by a cook and two waiters. Best of all were the observation-parlor cars, which included a back porch from which to watch the world slip over the horizon.

In an effort to provide every comfort offered by the steam railroads, a few interurbans even ran overnight trains with sleeping cars. This was a remarkable effort, considering that the interurbans traveled such short distances.

The Interstate Public Service Company ran sleeping cars over just 117 miles of track between Indianapolis and Louisville. The trip normally took less than four hours—not a very good night's rest. So the sleeping cars pulled out of town each night and then parked on a siding along the way! They resumed traveling before dawn so that passengers would arrive at the end of the tracks around breakfast time.

Typically, a trolley sleeping car had upper and lower beds that folded down on either side of the aisle, like bunk beds; during the day, the beds were folded up out of the way for seating. But the Illinois Traction System offered something better on its run between Peoria and Saint Louis. The cars had tiny bedrooms complete with toilets, hot and cold running water, vacuum bottles to hold ice water, fans, and desks. But as highways were improved, an automobile could travel between the two cities in just a few hours. By 1940, when these were the last interurban sleeping cars running in North America, they carried an average of less than two passengers per trip.

The interurbans not only gave city people a chance to visit

Not all trolleys stuck to land. The Sacramento Northern crossed broad Suisan Bay aboard a ferry, the Ramon.

the country; they made it possible for them to *live* there. Fast and frequent service could take them into town to work and shop. New towns quickly sprang up along interurban lines. In just ten years, seventeen were founded along the tracks of Los Angeles' Pacific Electric.

You can still spot these "trolley suburbs" around the country by looking for strings of houses built during the interurban years. A popular building style of the time was the bungalow, with its low roof. The tracks are long since gone, but the bungalow neighborhoods remain.

Safety

Most interurban lines had one track to handle trolleys traveling in two directions. The potential problems are obvious.

A remedy was to occasionally add a sidetrack, called a passing siding, where a train could duck out of the way and let the oncoming train continue. But how could a motorman know when to pull into the siding?

Steam railroads used fancy, expensive electric signaling systems. Few interurbans could afford that, and they came up with cheaper alternatives. One frugal line put its passing sidings on hills so that a motorman could see whether or not he could make it safely to the siding on the next hill. Another interurban used electric signals, but pieced together a system from ordinary switches and clear light bulbs. The result sounds like a school science project, but it worked well for many years.

Oncoming trolleys weren't the only danger. Just as bandits held up stagecoaches, they occasionally stopped an interurban to collect the conductor's nickels and the passengers' jewelry. Some thieves would block the tracks in a remote place and ambush the next car to come along. Others preferred to climb on top of a car, yank down the trolley pole, and wait for the car to coast to a stop.

The Beginning of the End

The automobile and the interurban are twins. Both were born at the close of the 1800s. Cars were impractical playthings at the time; the roads were so bad that their great speed only got them into trouble. Instead, it was the quiet, smooth, and smokeless interurban that impressed people as the vehicle of the future.

Trolleys have nearly vanished from the American landscape, but they helped to change that landscape beyond recognition. Here are three photos taken from the same spot in Philadelphia in 1900, 1908, and 1992, showing how a wobbly interurban line helped transform the world along the tracks.

The interurbans went on to become the most popular way of traveling in the United States, next to walking. Even though more and more automobiles were sold each year, interurban officials liked to call the car a fad, as if it were a silly hairstyle.

But the highways bled away ever greater numbers of passengers. Business turned bad in the 1920s, and then the United States entered the economic slump called the depression. People with small incomes had been the interurbans' best passengers because few could afford cars, and now they couldn't afford trolley tickets, either. In the 1930s, a thousand miles of track were ripped up each year, until only half of the web of interurban lines was left.

Several interurbans came out with fast, all-new equipment to lure people away from their automobiles. The Cincinnati and Lake Erie ran its 80-mile-per-hour cars, known as Red Devils, clear across Ohio. Speedy trains called Bullets were put in service on the Philadelphia and Western in Pennsylvania. The finest interurban trains ever built were the North Shore's Elec-

A PCC car rolls through a country landscape near Pittsburgh now covered with buildings.

The North Shore hoped its speedy, handsome Electroliners would bring passengers back to the interurban.

troliners, introduced in 1941. They were fast—capable of more than 100 miles per hour—and they looked it. Their streamlined front ends might have been something out of a comic book set in a future time. Waiters wore uniforms designed for the train. Even the hamburgers were special—they were called Electroburgers.

The Second World War, with its restrictions on the use of automobiles, sent millions of passengers back to railroads of all kinds. The tracks of the surviving interurbans were again very busy. One line, the Illinois Terminal Railroad, made the mistake of thinking the passengers had returned to stay. It spent a million dollars on three new streamlined, air-conditioned trains. Each ended with a dining-parlor-observation car that proudly bore the train's name on an illuminated sign.

But the Illinois Terminal's confidence was not rewarded. When cars and gasoline again became plentiful after the war, the crowds vanished. By 1956, the company put its three named trains up for sale. No buyer made an offer, and the cars were cut up for scrap metal.

The true interurbans are gone, but you can still ride lines out of Philadelphia that suggest what these railroads were like. This route to Media, a suburb, wanders over streams and through the woods.

Railroads evolve like animals, only much faster. The 1940 photo on the left shows a trolley between Baltimore and Annapolis, Maryland. Half a century earlier, these same tracks carried steam trains. And today, half a century later, they serve Baltimore's new light-rail line, shown on the right.

The last interurban, the proud North Shore, struggled on until 1963. And that was the end of this gracious way of traveling from one town to another, of escaping the house, of catching an evening breeze. It had taken just three decades for the interurbans to go from being the hottest things on wheels to rolling antiques. Perhaps no other business flowered and disappeared as quickly as the interurban railroads.

Does that mean the interurban was a waste of time and track? Not at all. It was the important link between beast-powered carts of past ages and the car in your driveway.

Light-Rail Vehicles

The interurban story doesn't end there. It might have, except that the enormous success of the automobile has led to enormous traffic jams. As fast as new highways are built, cars choke them.

That's not progress, and cities around North America have been looking for a way to move more people with less trouble. They believe they've found an answer—a vehicle that is quiet,

Faced with traffic congestion, the city of Portland, Oregon built a successful light-rail system instead of adding lanes to a highway.

puts off no exhaust, and can carry great gobs of passengers. A dozen cities have already built systems, and a dozen more are seriously considering them.

This vehicle happens to bear a very strong family resemblance to an interurban or streetcar. It's usually called a light-rail vehicle, or LRV for short. But that's only because *trolley* or *interurban* would sound too old-fashioned.

These shiny LRVs do have a few new tricks. They are air-conditioned, accelerate quickly, and often use computers for easier control. But a Rip Van Winkle, stepping aboard an LRV after a sleep of many years, wouldn't feel out of place in one of these reborn trolleys.

Light rail appeals to cities that don't want to spend the hundreds of millions of dollars needed to build a heavy-duty subway or ground-level railroad. And light-rail tracks can be tucked almost anywhere in a crowded city—in tunnels, over old railroad lines, and even through city streets.

CHAPTER 6

Subways and Elevated Trains

In cities, where a square foot of ground can be worth millions of dollars, land is often too valuable for railroad tracks. So city trains have been sent up into the air on elevated tracks (or "els"), and down into the ground in subway tunnels.

Above: Charles Harvey rode in a railcar to demonstrate that his invention, the first elevated railroad, really worked.
(New York Transit Authority)

60

These trains are often lumped together as "rapid transit." They aren't necessarily more rapid than trains that run along the ground. But the name has been around for a century and it isn't likely to be changed.

Even though they cost far more to build than railroads on the ground, subways and elevated trains are still with us—decades after most streetcar and interurban lines have vanished. The automobile has failed to kill off rapid transit. In fact, four times as many cities in North America have rapid transit systems today as back in the 1930s. These trains are still the best way we've found to move a lot of people in a crowded place.

The Train As a Bird

An elevated railroad travels in a world of its own. Tracks, control towers, and stations are high above the crowds and traffic. The trains hover above the city like low-flying helicopters. They don't have to slow for pedestrians and other vehicles, and their tracks can be bustling places. A crossing of two elevated lines in Chicago is said to have been the busiest rail intersection in the world—at certain times of day, a train roared past every 8½ seconds.

The first successful elevated railroad began running above the streets of New York City in 1870. Cars were hauled down the tracks by a cable, an awkward form of propulsion that was replaced by small steam engines. The line was a success, and others followed. But a steam engine throws off cinders and sparks, and many people weren't happy about their messy new neighbor in the sky.

The man who had been responsible for developing the

Left: Above the striped awnings of shops, trains travel Chicago's elevated rail system a hundred years ago.

Below: Many years later, a modern elevated train skims over the streets of Chicago.

This elevated train avoids the busy Philadelphia streets below.

electric streetcar, Frank Sprague, came up with a better way to run rapid transit trains. He invented what are known as multiple-unit cars, each with its own electric motors and each with controls for running all the cars of a train at once. That way, a train can be made up quickly, with any number of cars hooked together in any order.

Elevated railroads have their problems, however, and many cities have ripped them out altogether. The tracks block out the sun and sky for people who already may feel hemmed in by tall buildings. The streets below can be dark and unappealing. Elevated trains also broadcast their noise more than their cousins on the ground and below it.

But Chicago's old els still are important to the city. And tracks continue to be built into the air, with more care taken

The tall, graceful pillars of Vancouver's Skytrain have little in common with the black iron land-bridges of earlier els.

A Washington Metro train passes John F. Kennedy Stadium.
It will duck underground as it enters the crowded capital city.

that they won't be in the way of people living below. Much of the track branching from the Washington, D.C.–area Metro is elevated. Toronto has its elevated Scarborough Rapid Transit line. In Vancouver, British Columbia, the Skytrain travels as a subway under the city and then changes personalities as it leaps dramatically into the air.

The Train As a Worm

Cities make good use of the space below their streets. The earth is a convenient place to tuck water lines, sewer pipes, wires, warehouses—and trains.

The first subway in North America was built under the streets of New York by an inventor named Alfred Beach. A lot of dirt and rock would have to be dealt with. Worse, Beach knew he would have to deal with the state's most powerful crook, William Tweed.

*New York's peashooter subway propelled its cylindrical car
with a huge fan.*

Tweed was a politician who quietly received money from
New York's horsecar and omnibus lines for helping them do
business. He nearly persuaded New York State to tear down
the city's first elevated line, and Beach guessed the man would
not be enthusiastic about a new subway. Still, Beach was con-
fident that once he opened a short experimental line, riders
would love it so much that the state would have to approve of
his plans.

But first he had to build the line—and that would have to
be done in secret. Workers got to work in 1868, digging from
the basement of a clothing store. They tunneled by day, when
the sounds of their shovels were masked by carriages traveling

above. By night, they slipped dirt and rock out of the building.

Since he had never seen a subway before, Beach was free to dream up a splendid one. The single can-shaped car didn't have a motor. Instead, it fit snugly in its tunnel and would be blown along its tube like a pea out of a straw. An enormous steam-powered fan would provide the breath for this pneumatic system. The car was fitted with comfortable couches. The station from which passengers departed had paintings on the walls, a piano, a decorative fountain, and even tanks for goldfish.

The entire plan sounded like something from a science-fiction story. But the line worked, and it was a hit with the public when revealed in 1870. Some 400,000 passengers paid a quarter for a ride the length of a football field, when tickets above ground cost just a nickel or two. Here was a way to travel

The first practical subway in North America was a tunnel that carried streetcars below Boston's streets. Here, a streetcar drops out of sight as it heads downtown.

Manhattan without dust, mud, bumps, noise, traffic jams, and horse waste. Beach promised that the completed subway would blow along at 60 miles per hour—at a time when horsecars were averaging less than six.

Boss Tweed wasn't pleased about the secret subway. When state lawmakers voted to allow the line to be lengthened, Tweed ordered the governor to kill the project.

Beach went broke. His subway was abandoned. The little tunnel was used as a wine cellar for a time, and then as a shooting gallery. Finally, New York's grandest transportation system was sealed up forever.

The Old Tunnels of New York

Alfred Beach died without knowing that New York would go on to build the largest subway system in the world. It has also been called the dirtiest, the noisiest, and the scariest.

A New York subway is a lot like a roller coaster. The ride is so bumpy and loud that you feel as though the train could leave the track at any minute. But while a roller coaster offers dizzying heights, New York's subways stun passengers by taking them to different worlds within minutes. For example, if you get on the Lexington Avenue line in midtown and head north, you may notice a remarkable number of passengers wearing baseball gloves—the train stops just outside the walls of Yankee Stadium.

Or head south, and the car takes on many East Asian people, as if you've traveled straight through the planet and come out the other side. Get off at Canal Street and your nose solves the mystery: The smell of fresh fish and spices from the China-

Above: City and transit officials visited New York's City Hall Station shortly after it was built. The skylights glowed with light admitted by small glass discs set in the sidewalk far above. (New York Transit Archives, Brooklyn N.Y.)

Left: Many of New York's subway stations have pictures in tile that celebrate the history of the neighborhood. The mosaic beaver at Astor Place recalls that John Jacob Astor made a fortune selling beaver pelts to the hat industry. Photo by David Lubarsky. (New York Transit Archives, Brooklyn, N.Y.)

town markets and restaurants wafts down through the sidewalk grates.

Unfortunately, tunnels tend to collect undesirable things. Water, for one. Subways often are damp and musty. Dirt, for another. Without wind and rain to scrub them, older subways can resemble the inside of a smokestack. Subway tunnels may also attract animals and people that aren't welcomed above ground. Rats feed off of litter. In much the same way, criminals feed off of other people. And others take advantage of the dark to paint graffiti, the symbols and signatures with which people have been decorating public places for centuries.

Not everyone thinks of graffiti as a problem. One New York magazine called the colorful paintings the true art of our time. Graffiti makers have been invited to show their work in the city's art galleries. But transit officials found that graffiti makes riders feel the subway system is out of control.

New York's subway system found a solution to the problem. The cure sounds simple, but it worked: No car was allowed out on the tracks if it was marked up. Crews set upon the designs with brushes and strong chemical solvents. Before long, the artists lost interest in making paintings they would never see again.

In spite of their place in the damp basement of transportation, subways are too important to be done away with. Every other type of railroad has lost miles of track over the years—steam, cable, interurban, streetcar, elevated—but North America's subway mileage continues to grow. The reason is that subways make a city more livable. Toronto calculated that if it didn't build a subway, an extra 122,000 automobiles would pour into the city, requiring thirty-five new highway lanes.

*Above: In a successful campaign, New York City subway cars were
scrubbed to discourage graffiti painters.* (New York Transit Archives,
Brooklyn, N.Y.)

*Below: New, clean cars can be pleasant to ride. This car is in use on
the Washington Metro.*

Note the round lights set into the platform of this Washington Metro station. They normally glow dull orange. But the lights silently announce that a train is coming by growing brighter and then pulsing intensely.

New subways have learned from the problems of older lines. Washington's Metro stations are enormous, arching vaults that don't need a cluster of columns to support the ceiling, and television cameras are able to scan these open spaces for would-be criminals. The walls curve out of reach from the passenger platform, making it more difficult to ornament them

The Lindenwold line was one of the first rapid transit systems built to compete with the automobile. A train crosses the Ben Franklin Bridge into Camden, New Jersey.

with graffiti. Even the stations are air-conditioned, so passengers don't feel they are on a journey to the center of the earth.

Toronto uses huge skylights to brighten its Glencairn subway station. And subway cars in Montreal and Mexico City run on rubber tires. Their big advantage is what's missing—the noise for which subways have always been famous.

Trains with Brains

The newest rapid transit systems are apt to be missing something else: a driver. The first rapid transit trains to drive themselves were set loose in 1969 on the Lindenwold line between Philadelphia and Camden, New Jersey, and BART (Bay Area Rapid Transit), centered in San Francisco. Since then, driverless trains have gone into service in several other cities. On some lines, an operator is on board to watch over the train, while allowing computers to do most of the work. But the Skytrain in Vancouver has no one in the cab at all.

You might guess it would feel uncomfortable to let a box of electronic parts take you on an 80-mile-per-hour ride. But in fact, most commercial airline flights are run in part by "automatic pilots," at far greater speeds. And few of us think twice about stepping into an automatic elevator, which whisks us hundreds of feet above the ground.

CHAPTER 7

Commuter Trains

Are you a commuter? Probably. A commuter is anyone who travels to work or school from home each day. Commuters tend to travel at two particular times—during morning and late-afternoon rush hours. Since the 1800s, railroads have run special commuter trains to carry these tides of people.

A commuter train travels a short distance because few commuters are willing to make daily trips of much more than eighty miles. And it tends to be a plain, vanilla sort of train because few commuters want to take the time and pay extra to eat, drink, and relax in dining and lounge cars.

Above: An electric train drops off tired New York commuters in suburban Connecticut.

A rail diesel car, or RDC, carries its own diesel motor, and is cheaper to run than a locomotive-drawn train.

Suburban Arteries

Like trolleys, the commuter trains of the steam railroads helped create the suburbs they ran through. As tracks spread out of a city, people moved to new communities along the line. Houses appeared like huge crops in what had been farm fields. These new towns have been called "bedroom communities" because they provide homes for people who work and shop someplace else.

Unlike most long-distance trains, commuter trains often ran on electricity. Steam engines put off clouds of smoke and poisonous gases, and cities weren't happy about letting these rolling smokestacks come into the heart of town. Electric locomotives not only were nonsmokers, but also terrifically powerful. That meant more cars could be hauled over crowded tracks. They were cheaper to run, too—the steam locomotive gobbled more fuel to carry each passenger a mile than any other vehicle except the airplane.

The Great City Stations

Many commuter trains ran out of huge city stations built by North America's steam railroads. These buildings were among the finest ever seen in North America. The architects who designed them had high goals. The stations didn't just keep passengers warm and dry; they were intended to lift the human spirit. For that reason, the great stations were patterned after the cathedrals and castles of Europe.

New York's Grand Central Terminal has been called the greatest station of them all. The main waiting area may be the most famous room in the United States. It is big enough to hold a football field and high enough that the ball probably wouldn't touch the ceiling. The ceiling itself is famous. It is painted with constellations—animals and people from old myths that are sketched each night by the stars. The huge pictures are made up of twenty-five hundred painted stars, the brightest sixty of which glow with electric lights.

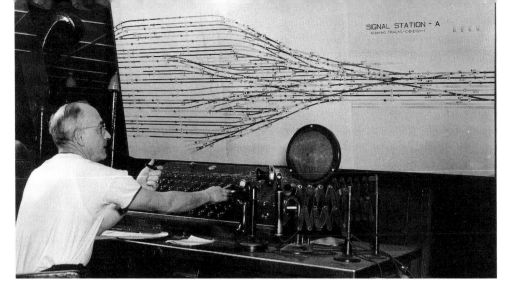

*Above: The tides of trains that sweep in and out of New York's Grand
Central Station are controlled from underground offices called "towers."
Each line on the map represents a set of tracks.*

*Below: A favorite view of photographers is the play of light as it cuts
through Grand Central.*

A Business Nobody Wants

Running commuter trains is not a profitable business. Nearly a hundred years ago, commuter trains already were losing passengers to trolleys. Commuters often have had to put up with old equipment and poor service.

The railroads got rid of many of their commuter trains to save money. City and state governments were forced to take over the few trains that were left. But government help doesn't guarantee that trains will keep running. The price you pay for a ticket may cover less than half the cost of your ride. The

The engineer of this electric commuter train chats with a trainman, as passengers walk into Philadelphia's Reading Terminal. The overhead train shed roof is gone, now that trains use a modern underground station.

remaining amount has to be approved by voters and politicians. For that reason, commuter trains can disappear overnight. This unreliable service is frustrating to people who are willing to leave their cars at home and buy a ticket.

Commuter trains are worth saving. They can beat highways and even airlines as the fastest way into a city or from one city to another. And so it is that new commuter systems are being planned or built in more than a dozen North American cities. The lines aren't expected to make money. But these cities realize that people can't live comfortably without them.

A Caltrans commuter train stops at the traditional-looking station at Menlo Park, California.

CHAPTER 8

City Trains for a New Century

Two steel rails, laid side by side, were once the hottest thing in transportation. And then the railroad became old news, and those rails looked like rusty relics from another age.

Above: Germany's Wuppertal monorail may be the only railroad in the world to travel up a river.

This baby trolley scoots across the campus of West Virginia University. The tiny cars have no drivers. You push a button along the tracks, and a computer-guided car stops to take you to your destination.

Today, that same simple idea—steel wheels rolling on steel rails—is exciting once again. Cities around the world are proud of their new light-rail and rapid transit systems. But a pair of rails isn't the only way to support a train. There are railroads that use just one rail, called monorails. And other trains, riding on magnets, don't touch the ground at all!

Monorails, Yesterday's Train of the Future

Monorails were the trains of the future a century ago, and people still talk about them that way. Maybe that's because they look like something from a Jetsons cartoon. Whether the trains hang down from their single rail or straddle it like a person riding a horse, monorails seem odd. Dozens of cities have talked about building them. But in North America, the plans have come to nothing. A more ordinary type of transportation always wins.

Monorails shouldn't seem so strange. A line has been operating for ninety years in Wuppertal, Germany. In the United States, millions of people have ridden the short monorails at Disneyland and Walt Disney World, as well as a one-mile line built to serve a fair in Seattle. Unlike the Wuppertal, North

The quiet electric cars of the Disney World monorail
pass right through a hotel lobby.

*Built for the Seattle World's Fair, this monorail
continues to run on its double-track line.*

America's three monorails ride on top of the rail. The Japanese lead the world in monorails, with several lines. One passes through tunnels to avoid climbing hills along its route. Another will be twenty-five miles long—the longest monorail ever built—when completed.

Like an elevated railroad, a monorail runs without interfering with life down at ground level. The rail and the supporting posts are less expensive to build than heavy elevated tracks and block less of the sky. The Wuppertal line glides above a river, the only place in the crowded town that a railroad could be squeezed. Its cars hang down from their overhead track, and that looks a little daring. Still, in all of those years of operation, there have been no fatal accidents—just a *famous* accident. A baby circus elephant named Tuffi rode the train as a stunt. She became frightened and leaped from the train before anyone could stop her. Fortunately, Tuffi landed safely in the river.

What is it like to ride a monorail? The view is excellent. There aren't any tracks or railings to get in the way. Some lines have rubber tires for a smooth ride. But monorails do feel a little different from anything else on wheels. The ones that hang from the rail are free to tilt to the side as they round corners, somewhat like a yo-yo being swung in a circle. Some riders find that they feel mildly seasick from the experience.

Are monorails safe? So far, no one has ever been killed in a monorail accident. But each line has to work out a way to rescue passengers from cars that have broken down or caught on fire. On some monorails, another train comes from behind to help. Passengers go out the back of their train to the rescue train. On double-track lines, they take a deep breath to settle

The only maglev train in regular use is Britain's short line serving the Birmingham airport.

their nerves, then cross on a short emergency bridge to a train on the other track.

Trains That Float on Magnets

For a hundred years, trains were the fastest vehicles on earth. They've since lost the speed race to airplanes. But that may change, according to scientists working on something called magnetic levitation.

Have you ever noticed how one magnet repels another so that the magnet on top seems to float weightlessly? Researchers have floated entire railroad trains with that same principle, using huge magnets. There is a practical reason for this magic trick. A train that floats isn't slowed by the friction from wheels or rails, and speeds of nearly 300 miles per hour have been reached in test runs. The trains are also propelled by magnets pushing and pulling them along. These remarkable motors are nearly silent and have no moving parts to break or wear down.

Magnetic levitation (or maglev, for short) was invented in the early 1900s by Robert Goddard, a man whom we remember instead for having dreamed up the solid-fuel rocket. But Germany and Japan have now taken the lead in maglev research. Why? It has been said that Americans are so used to slow train travel that they wouldn't feel comfortable at the great speeds magnetic levitation might make possible. Just as early train passengers feared their bodies would explode, we may have an irrational fear about traveling over the ground at 300 miles per hour. Jet airliners go faster, of course, but at such a high altitude that you have little sensation of speed.

Now in the planning stage are maglev trains that will travel several hundred miles per hour.

There are plans for a German company to build what may be the world's first maglev railroad, between the airport at Orlando, Florida, and nearby Disney World. But the Japanese are also at work on their own line; if the trains run as planned, they should be the world's fastest in regular service, at 300 miles per hour.

Some transportation people don't see why maglevs cause such a fuss. They point out that the familiar steel-wheeled train has gone over 400 miles per hour in tests. Why bother inventing new technologies?

The reason, according to researchers, is that far greater speeds are possible. Maglev trains may someday float their way across the continent in tubes from which the air is pumped. By traveling in this near vacuum, they wouldn't be slowed by wind resistance, and could conceivably reach 3,000 miles per hour!

For now, supersonic trains are little more than sketches on paper. But these fresh ideas are the latest example of the railroad's remarkable ability to cast off a rusty, obsolete skin and reappear as a brand-new machine. The train will keep evolving to serve future generations living in cities we can only imagine. And if the cars still have windows and that old-fashioned restful swaying, the ride promises to be fun.

TO FIND OUT MORE

Magazines

The New Electric Railway Journal, 717 Second Street, N.E. Washington, DC 20002.

Electric Lines, 77 West Nicholai Street, Hicksville, NY 11801.

Trains, PO Box 1612, Waukesha, WI 53187.

Books

Here is a sampling of recommended books. Many books on city trains are published by small companies, and may be hard to find at your local library or bookstore.

Autokind vs. Mankind, by Kenneth R. Schneider. New York: W. W. Norton, 1971. A study of how people are affected by the transportation systems they choose.

The Cable Car in America, by George W. Hilton. Berkeley, California: Howell-North Books, 1971.

The Electric Interurban Railways in America, by George W. Hilton and John F. Due. Stanford, California: Stanford University Press, 1960.

From Bullets to BART. Central Electric Railfans' Association, PO Box 503, Chicago, IL 60690. Photos of electric railways across the country, old and new.

A Guide to Chicago's Rapid Transit, by Richard Kunz. Andover, New Jersey: Andover Junction, 1991.

Indiana Railroad, Central Electric Railfans' Association, PO Box 503, Chicago, IL 60690.

Light Rail Transit on the West Coast, by Harre W. Demoro and John N. Harder. New York: Quadrant Press, 1989.

North Shore: America's Fastest Interurban, by William D. Middleton. San Marino, California: Golden West Books, 1964. An in-depth look at one of the most interesting and longest-lasting interurban lines.

A Rainbow of Traction. Central Electric Railfans' Association, PO Box 503, Chicago, IL 60690. Color photos of older city trains.

Red Arrow, by Ronald DeGraw. Glendale, California: Interurban Press, 1985. The story of a suburban Philadephia rail system.

The San Diego Trolley, by Gena Holle. Glendale, California: Interurban Press, 1990.

The Story of Metro: Transportation and Politics in the Nation's Capital, by Ronald H. Deiter. Glendale, California: Interurban Press, 1990.

Time of the Trolley, by William D. Middleton. San Marino, California: Golden West Books, 1987. An excellent general study, in words and photos.

Traction Handbook for Model Railroads, by Paul and Steven Mallery. 2-10-4 Publications, PO Box 16504, Fort Worth, TX 76162. How to build a model railroad of streetcars, trolleys, and other tiny city trains.

Under the Sidewalks of New York: The Story of the World's Greatest Subway System, by Brian J. Cudahy. New York: The Stephen Greene Press/Pelham Books, 1988.

Uptown, Downtown: A Trip Through Time on New York's Subways, by Stan Fischler. New York: Hawthorn/Dutton, 1976.

Videos

All videos are available from Transit Gloria Mundi, 36 East 27th Street, Baltimore, MD 21218.

Light Rail Panorama.

Ropes and Rails. San Francisco cable cars.

Trolley: The Cars That Built Our Cities.

Museums

Como-Harriet Streetcar Line, Minnesota Transportation Museum, PO Box 1796, Pioneer Station, Minneapolis, MN 55101.

Fort Smith Trolley Museum, 2121 Wolfe Lane, Fort Smith, AR 72901.

Illinois Railway Museum, PO Box 427, Union, IL 60180.

Iowa Trolley Park, PO Box 956, Mason City, IO 50401.

New York Transit Authority Museum, Boerum Place and Schermer-horn Street, Brooklyn, NY 11201

Pennsylvania Trolley Museum, PO Box 832, Pittsburgh,PA 15320

Rockhill Trolley Museum, PO Box 203, Rockhill Furnace, PA 17249.

Shelburne Falls Trolley Museum, 12 Water Street, Shelburne Falls, MA 01370.

The Valley Railroad Company, PO Box 452, Essex, CT 06426.

INDEX

ACKNOWLEDGMENTS

The author thanks William D. Middleton, who reviewed the manuscript; Terence W. Cassidy, librarian and information specialist with the Southeastern Pennsylvania Transportation Authority; Kathleen Collins, archivist with the New York Transit Authority; transit consultant George Krambles; Richard R. Kunz, editor of *The New Electric Railway Journal*; and railroad photographers Fred Schneider III and Ronald Karr.

Illustration credits: Title page and pages 36, 76, and 79, Ronald Karr; page 7, Warren Wing; page 10, Security Pacific National Bank Photograph Collection, Los Angeles Public Library; pages 14 and 29, Library of Congress; pages 15 and 16, Smithsonian Institution, negative numbers 610 A and 48181; page 19, Oregon Historical Society; pages 20 and 65, William D. Middleton; pages 21 and 82, Van Wilkins; pages 9, 12, 23, 38, 54, 63, 67, 71 (bottom), 72, and 84, Fred W. Schneider III; page 25, LeRoy O. King collection; page 27, S. E. Dohr collection; pages 32 (bottom) and 45, H. P. Sell/RTY Collection; pages 32 (top two photos), 49 (bottom), 57 (left), 62, 81, and 83, George Krambles collection; page 34, collection of Wayne C. Olsen; page 39, © 1983, Don Poggensee (Courtesy Gomaco Trolley Company); page 40, Donald Duke collection; pages 47 and 49 (top), John P. Shuman; page 51, Arthur Alter photo, W. S. Billings collection; page 52 (top two photos), Hagley Museum and Library; page 53 (bottom), A. Eht Tem collection; page 55, John Gruber; page 56, Donald R. Kaplan, courtesy of Ronald DeGraw; page 57 (right) William S. Lind, *The New Electric Railway Journal*; page 58, Harold Underdown; page 64, BC Transit; page 66, State Historical Society of Wisconsin; page 73, Carlton Road, Delaware River Port Authority, Camden, New Jersey; page 75, author's collection; page 78 (top), David V. Hyde, from New York Central System Historical Society collection; page 78 (bottom), Ed Nowak, from New York Central System Historical Society collection; page 80, Bob Colin photo, courtesy of Caltrans; page 86, Railway Gazette International; page 88, Transrapid International.